In memory of my grandmother, Bernice Carlson
—M.W.C.

For Michael, Erin, and Ryan
—J.T.

The artist would like to thank the
Steamtown National Historic Site in Scranton, Pennsylvania,
and the Railroad Museum of Pennsylvania in Strasburg
for their assistance

Prairie Train   Text copyright © 2003 by Marsha Wilson Chall   Illustrations copyright © 2003 by John Thompson
Manufactured in China. All rights reserved.   www.harperchildrens.com

Library of Congress Cataloging-in-Publication Data   Chall, Marsha Wilson.   Prairie train / by Marsha Wilson Chall ; illustrations by John Thompson.   p.   cm.
Summary: A young girl experiences the thrill of her first train ride when she takes the Great Northern from the country to visit her grandmother in the city.
ISBN 0-688-13433-5 — ISBN 0-688-13434-3 (lib. bdg.)   [1. Railroads—Trains—Fiction.   2. Prairies—Fiction.]   I. Thompson, John, 1940– ill.   II. Title.
PZ7. C3496 Pr   2003   2001024965

Typography by Carla Weise 1 2 3 4 5 6 7 8 9 10 ❖ First Edition

PRAIRIE TRAIN

by MARSHA WILSON CHALL ⬤ *illustrations by* JOHN THOMPSON

HarperCollinsPublishers

Shhh, listen—
Here she comes—*woooOOOO!*
In the dark I stretch full-out,
my ear down to the floor.
Clackety clack clack clack.
The Great Northern rumbles
over frozen tracks.
Her headlight sweeps across the field;
broken cornstalks wave
hellooOOOO. . . .
Night chases close behind her
and hitches a rail.
So LOOOoong . . .

Next morning at the station,

Mama spit-combs my bangs.

"All abooaard!" shouts the conductor.

"Go on now," says Mama.

"Grandma's waiting on the other end."

The conductor pulls me up the high, metal steps.

My patent-leather shoes gleam,

as smooth as the steel rails below.

Shooh . . .

    Shooh . . .

The engine pants and huffs

and puffs a cloud of steam.

Mama walks alongside waving,

then runs to keep up.

I press my nose against the glass.

"Hurry, Mama," I call to her,

but she can't hear me.

So many windows, they let in the sky!
The sun breaks into pieces
on a rose-garden carpet.
I ride on a throne of velvet,
on cushions as soft as caterpillars,
brass fittings polished to gold;
here on the Great Northern
heading far away from home—
    shined shoes,
        white gloves,
           coin purse,
              two dollars,
                  cranberry coat,
                    wool beret—
                        Grandma's girl,
                        city queen.

The prairie is stitched together
in brown and yellow patches,
like Grandma's quilt spread over the hills.
An old windmill spins like a crazy Ferris wheel.
A silo stretches, tight with winter feed.
I wave hello to Holstein cows
and read the sides of barns:

LOG CABIN SYRUP—FINE QUALITY SINCE 1887

USE GOLD MEDAL FLOUR, NATURE'S BEST

LAY OR BUST POULTRY FEEDS

The woman facing me knits—
clickety click click click—
keeping time with the Great Northern line.

"First call for dinner."
A waiter plays the chimes.
I wade across the swaying floor
and hold my breath between the cars.
The tablecloths are bright as snow,
with red carnations in the middle.
The silverware is shined so high,
I can count my teeth in it,
send signals with it,
look behind me in it.
Beside the crystal salt and pepper,
sugar cubes are piled up in a china bowl.
In my head, I hear Mama:
"No playing with your food."
I check behind me
in my silver-knife mirror,
then build a ten-story sugar-cube tower.
The waiter shows me the menu;
I order just what I like,
then open my napkin and wait.

"Thank you," I say,

and eat the cherries from the fruit cocktail,

crumble crackers in the chicken noodle soup,

then sip my hot cocoa

till the foam is all gone.

I dab my mouth with the big white napkin

so the waiter will know that I'm done.

"Still room for Neapolitan ice cream?"

He swoops my plate away.

"Yes, please," I tell him,

then open my new coin purse

and drop in five sugar cubes.

Between Parker's Lake and Glena,
it starts to snow,
frosting the fields,
coating the cows.
Their black patches disappear—
ghost cows.
Ice pings at my window
like glass beads unstrung.
The hay bales are white
and as round as igloos.
A stop sign stops no one—
the snow has erased the road.
But the Great Northern plows on,
rolling, rolling, rolling.

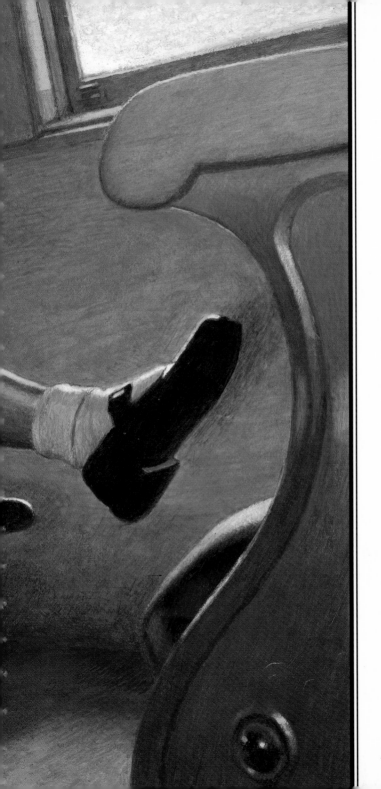

Clickety click click click
go the woman's needles,
keeping time—
then stop.
The brakes moan, the cars lurch.
I tumble onto the carpet.
My coin purse slides beneath the seat.
"Porter?" she calls.
"A snowdrift, ma'am. We can't get through."
She helps me up and hands me my coin purse.
I shove it deep in my pocket.

The Great Northern is as quiet
as a frozen buffalo.
I listen to the north wind chase and snap
all around us,
and button my coat
clear up to my neck.
"Grandma's waiting on the other end,"
I can hear Mama say.
But how long will she wait?
The woman picks up her needles.
Clickety click click click.
Snowbound time
on the Great Northern line.

"Would you like to try?" she asks.

"Don't know how," I say.

She pats the empty seat beside her—

knit one,

purl two,

yellow yarn,

corn rows,

fingers flutter,

snow falls—

Grandma's girl,

knitting queen.

The prairie is dark

and the cold sneaks in,

and Grandma is waiting.

How long will she wait?

A tall boy wearing a tie

takes out a silver harmonica.

Before I can think, I am singing

"Oh! Susanna" and

"The Ballad of Casey Jones,"

then "Can't you hear the captain shouting . . ."

Shhh, listen—

WooOOOO!

In the aisle, I stretch full-out,

my ear down to the floor.

Rumble, rumble, rumble . . .

"Here it comes!" I shout.

A snowplow engine is tunneling through.

I blow on the glass and rub a peekhole.

Her firebox glows;

her headlight searches.

The snow flies—

we're saved!

This prairie train is city-bound again.

"My stop is next," says the knitting lady.
I help her carry her bags to the door,
where she folds down my collar
and straightens my beret.
Back in my seat,
I press my face against the glass.
"Wait, ma'am, you left your afghan!"
She waves as the train rolls forward.
"Good-bye, knitting lady. Good-bye!"

WooOOOO!
Clackety clack clack clack.
The prairie is stitched together
in brown and yellow patches
spread over my knees.
Fields start to sparkle
with lights of towns along the line—
Jordan . . .
Clayton . . .
Eastbend . . .

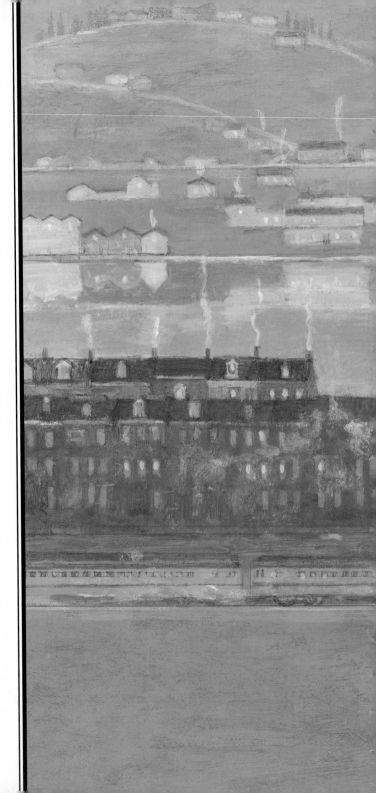

Then buildings and steeples and towers are flying by
in a city of lights,
zillions more than stars.
"St. Paul Union Depot!" the conductor shouts.
The engine sighs into her winter cave.
I press my nose against the glass—
"There she is!" I yell, and wave.
Grandma has waited
and I am ready,
riding on a throne of velvet,
on cushions as soft as caterpillars,
brass fittings polished to gold,
here on the Great Northern
far away from home—

shined shoes,
white gloves,
coin purse,
one dollar,
cranberry coat,
wool beret,
yellow afghan,
sugar cubes—
Grandma's girl,
city queen.